THE TIPTOEING TIGER

Philippa Leathers

WALKER BOOKS
AND SUBSIDIARIES
LONDON · BOSTON · SYDNEY · AUCKLAND

Everyone in the forest knew that tigers were sleek, silent and totally terrifying. When a tiger prowled through the forest, everyone found other places to be.

But no one took any notice
of Little Tiger.

No one jumped when he roared.

No one ran away when he tumbled through the forest.

His brother laughed. "Oh, Little Tiger, you're too small and clumsy to scare anyone!"

"I am not!" said Little Tiger. "I'm sleek, silent and totally terrifying."

His brother smiled. "I don't think you can scare a single animal in the forest."

"I can!" said Little Tiger. "And I'll prove it."

Little Tiger began to tiptoe through the forest as silently as he could.

Tiptoe, tiptoe, tiptoe ...

ROAR!!!

"You don't scare me," yawned Boar. "I could hear you coming a mile away."

"Bother!" said Little Tiger, and he set off again to find someone else to scare.

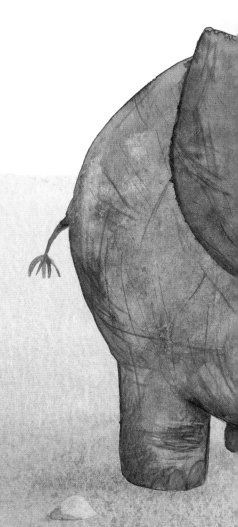

Tiptoe, tiptoe, tiptoe ...

"Hello, Little Tiger," said Elephant.
"Did I scare you?" asked Little Tiger.
"Oh, no. You're much too small."
"Bother!" said Little Tiger, and he set off again
to find someone else to scare.

Tiptoe, tiptoe, tiptoe ...

ROAR!

"Was that meant to scare us?" asked the
 monkeys, laughing.
"Yes, it was," said Little Tiger.
 The monkeys just kept laughing.

Little Tiger felt sad. *I may not be sleek, silent or totally terrifying,* he thought. *But I WILL find someone to scare!*

Just then a frog jumped – *SPLOSH!* – into a pond. *This is my chance*, thought Little Tiger. *I can scare that tiny, jumpy frog.*

He crept silently up to the water's edge.

Tiptoe, tiptoe, tiptoe ...

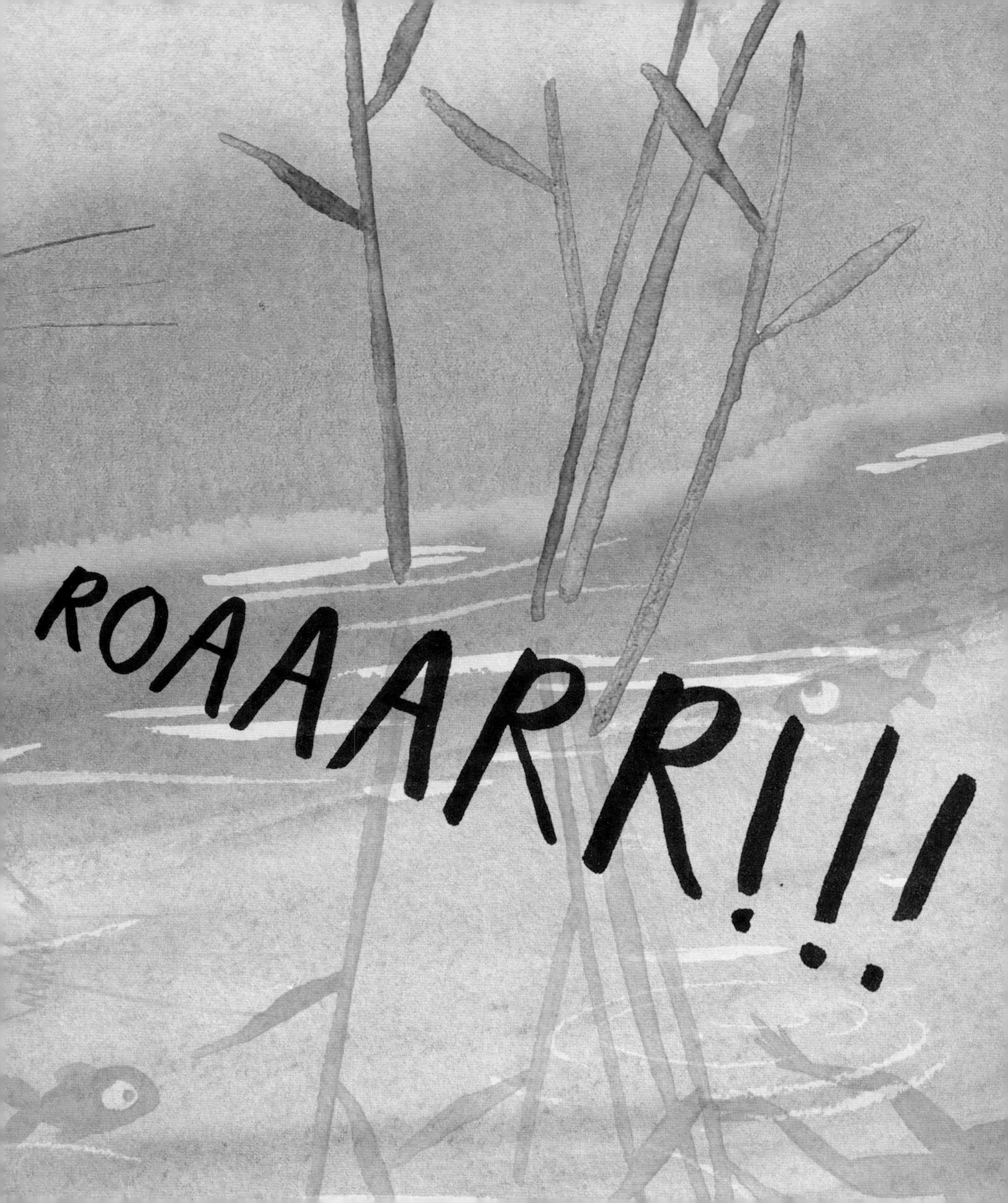
ROAAARR!!!

"Oh, help!" cried Little Tiger.

Bravely, Little Tiger tiptoed back to the water's edge and slowly peered into the pond.

A tiger – sleek, silent and totally terrifying – peered back.

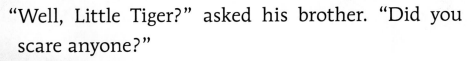

"Well, Little Tiger?" asked his brother. "Did you scare anyone?"

"As a matter of fact, I did," said Little Tiger.

"Myself!"

FOR ROWAN!!!

First published 2018 by Walker Books Ltd
87 Vauxhall Walk, London SE11 5HJ

© 2018 Philippa Leathers

The right of Philippa Leathers to be identified as the
author and illustrator of this work has been asserted by her
in accordance with the Copyright, Designs and Patents Act 1988

This book has been typeset in ITC Mendoza Roman

Printed in China

British Library Cataloguing in Publication Data:
a catalogue record for this book is available from the British Library

ISBN 978-1-4063-7695-1

www.walker.co.uk